UNDERNEATH THE SURREAL STARSHINE

THE ANOMALY DUOLOGY
BOOK 1

JOHN P. WARREN

Copyright © 2024 by John P. Warren

Layout design and Copyright © 2024 by Next Chapter

Published 2024 by Next Chapter

Cover art by Jaylord Bonnit

This book is a work of fiction. Names, characters, places, and incidents are the product of the author's imagination or are used fictitiously. Any resemblance to actual events, locales, or persons, living or dead, is purely coincidental.

All rights reserved. No part of this book may be reproduced or transmitted in any form or by any means, electronic or mechanical, including photocopying, recording, or by any information storage and retrieval system, without the author's permission.

CHAPTER ONE

An incredibly beautiful young woman captivated the onlookers as she made her way down through a glitzy downtown Cleveland street. She was on her way to an upper-class bar to meet her boyfriend. This coupling outside of a renowned nightclub caught the eye of one such onlooker on the opposite side of the street as they unabashedly embraced and kissed. He was a middle-aged white man but still had a youthful look to him. His name was Robert. He was wearing black leather gloves; the one on his left hand appeared cumbersome. As Robert stared over at this affluent couple of African American origin, rage consumed his heart. He was jealous and begrudged them for how happy they must have felt, and he increasingly came to hate himself for feeling this way. He turned his head away in envy and continued walking down his side of the street until he stumbled on a drunk homeless man who was about a decade and a half his senior. He passed this poor unfortunate individual and then turned his head back to gaze at him with a pair of venomous eyes. "You filthy-arsed, lazy bum! Don't you have anything better to do than lie there wallowing in your own self-pity and filth?"

The man belched and replied, "Fuck off!"

The homeless man sounded as if he had an Irish accent, and Robert's ear detected this, so he kicked him in the leg. "Irish, eh? My parents came from Ireland, the good part of Ireland, Ulster, and they worked, unlike you and your Fenian kind."

He noticed that the Irish man had a bottle of whisky and was imbibing from it. He moved closer to him, took out his penknife, and pointed it at the homeless man's neck. Robert then grabbed the bottle and forced it into the man's mouth. "Since you like drowning your sorrows, take on this sorrow for size. My ancestors, being part of the British Empire, spun this great nation. We were white and Protestant, intelligent human beings, not like you. The inferior, like you, have infected this world and exploited this country with your own pathetic cultures. Only Anglo-Saxons should be here."

The homeless man's face was turning red. He coughed and vomited all over Robert's arm.

"You stupid drunk! See what you did!"

The homeless man started choking. Robert became even angrier. "I didn't tell you to stop!"

He forced the bottle into the homeless man's mouth as he tried to breathe, breaking one of his teeth in the process. The man tried to move and kick Robert. Robert knew he had had enough. "Just look at you, you glorify drunkenness! You can't even hold your liquor! You might as well be a junkie gangster! I guess you will keep drinking yourself until you start singing and lamenting about your troubles! You good-for-nothing idiot!" Robert laughed as he yelled into the homeless man's face.

Hatred enveloped the ominous night air as Robert cleared

his throat and made a disgusting noise with his mouth. It sounded as if he was building up saliva, and indeed that's what he did. He moved over to the homeless man, and the man, realising what was coming, tried frantically to duck but could not. As Robert moved closer to this man's mouth, he unleashed a pile of dirty spit on the man's lips. This unsuspecting victim, being too drunk to taste how revolting it was due to his high alcohol intake that evening, tried to wipe the mucus from his mouth as it dripped down to his chin and stared at the unusual shining and sparkling dust in the summer dusky sky. He pondered as he gazed at the remnant of the Betelgeuse star and thought how another human being, like the man before him, could treat someone in such a disdainful manner and self-impose the right to play judge, jury, and executioner all in one go in such a short space of time and inflict decadent punishment like this.

Robert smirked at him and went on his way. He too looked up and thought about how the Betelgeuse star went nova over sixty years ago and how everyone marvelled at the night sky with wonder and caution over this new celestial occurrence. He was not an appreciator of the arts but conceded that it now glowed majestically and had a bright purple effulgence which captivated the minds of people, even those with minimal imagination like him. He then wondered why a strange cloud between the Earth and Mars was simply referred to by the media as the Anomaly. It was too menacing. The fact that he had just degraded a helpless member of society never registered again in his mind. He went to his station wagon and opened the door. He took off the gloves and rubbed his left hand. His left arm was slightly shorter than his right since birth.

This man, Robert Emerson, was a detestable person. Not just for nefarious deeds such as spitting on homeless people but for much worse. He was the type of man who was seemingly chosen by God for some profound act and thus protected by the devil and carried out both of their deeds, good and bad, accordingly, whether he lived his life sacrosanct or nefarious, which constantly paradoxed and contradicted each other, but always in a state of flux. Because he had no moral compass to keep all of this in balance, it fluctuated. Today he was evil.

He was middle-aged and had been single all his life. In fact, Robert Emerson was a full-blown fascist. He hated everyone that was not white or Protestant, like his father, who hailed from Northern Ireland. This hatred was paradoxical, however, as his mother also originated from there, only she was Catholic, and he had strong affection towards her. Both of his parents had now passed, but their respective influences always instilled separate values in him. His mother was more balanced than his father, but his father's influence was indeed stronger. She was the person who designed these handmade gloves for him to hide his infirmity. That is why he had such strong affection towards her, even in his memories of her now.

Robert watched an African American activist on the TV called Theodore Brooks on a current affairs show. Brooks was debating the current Black Lives Matter movement. Robert spat on his carpet when Brooks told the host: "We're all God's children." Robert had had an extremely negatively filled day so far. He hated watching the news, but to him, it was unavoidable. He hated watching it because of the cosmopolitan range of presenters it featured, or so he thought. And as the anger infused his blood with rage, he knew one thing, and that was to take down Theodore Brooks.

The sound of the AM radio band being scanned on a simple portable receiver slightly irritated Robert this sunny morning with its crackle and hum. Robert hurried to his basement to plug in his own assembled radio transmitter. He constantly changed the frequencies and even location of the transmitter to avoid the FCC from tracking him down throughout his hometown of Cleveland, Ohio. He was a pirate broadcaster spreading hate speech over the airwaves as well as online. There was considerable interference all over the radio nowadays. He did not realise its source, but it was in fact coming from that anomaly near the Earth.

Robert had the new frequency set to 750 KHz. Right away he began to play provocative music and then his daily rant. He spoke derogatorily about Theodore Brooks but didn't reveal his intention to wipe him out. He decided to assault his character first. As the barrage of castigating comments left Robert's angry lips, the listeners, if any, could visualise how pissed off this man was. An image of a raging, disgruntled, and envious, crazy, rabid hound must have been conveyed in their minds. This torrential diatribe from Robert Emerson would have even turned away his avid followers due to how uneasy he sounded.

CHAPTER
TWO

On this starry night, Robert couldn't help noticing how menacing the Anomaly looked in the bright sky. His moment of loathing was interrupted when he saw a pretty Asian woman in her thirties walking into the house that the Hendersons had vacated over four months ago. He couldn't help noticing how attractive she looked but immediately halted any wanting of her because of her race. This made him sad, and this was something that he would never admit to himself. On his way into his house, he heard her mother call her inside. He heard her name; it was Jessica. In his home, Robert had just downed and finished half a bottle of Scotch and hit the bed. He was out cold. He heard someone calling out to him, "Rob, Rob!"

He always hated being called by the shorter version of his name as he believed it to be improper. He got up from the bed and noticed everything was different in his house. For a start, it was clean and tidy, with all his belongings neatly arranged, and there was no sign of that empty bottle of Scotch he had finished hours earlier. As he proceeded to find the person who was calling out to him, he saw a suit in the wardrobe. It appeared expensive, and he knew he could never afford such fancy apparel. Someone was coming up the stairs. Robert quickly went out of the bedroom to see who it was. First, his instincts led him to look for his handgun, only it wasn't there – he woke up!

"What the fuck was that about?" he asked himself. It was about 7 a.m., and he decided that now he was awake, he would begin his day. He made an unhealthy breakfast consisting of burned bacon and sausages. He was about to close his eyes and yawn when his cell phone rang. He grabbed it from the table and looked at its display to see who was calling him this early but didn't recognise the number. He hesitated only because he felt a little braver than yesterday and quickly decided to answer the call.

"Hello?" he asked the caller.

"Is this Robert Emerson?"

"Who wants to know?"

"An inspired new follower. I heard your broadcasts over the last week. You really hit the issues on the head. I want to contribute. Can we meet up?"

Robert took a deep breath and decided to chance it. "You better not be an undercover cop entrapping me or anything, 'cause I don't like being fucked with."

"Trust me. I'm no pig."

"Good. How about this afternoon?"

"Afternoon's good. When and where?"

"In St. Matthew's Park. I take it you already know what I look like from my website?"

"Yes, I do. I'll be there."

"What's your alias?"

"The Exterminator."

The morning passed without any high drama, considering

7

Robert Emerson was living off the official grid. He cleaned himself up and got into his old station wagon, heading to St. Matthew's Park. As he made his way there, the journey for him was typical. Typical in regards to how he would watch people who were not like him with disdain and hatred. He would squint his eyes in a manner that portrayed him to others as narrow-minded and irksome. He finally arrived at the park's entrance and gazed around, scanning the area for any potential dangers. He got out, locked the doors of his station wagon, and proceeded on a walk through the park.

About half an hour passed when a young man bearing a skinhead approached him. "Are you Leader Emerson?"

"Who wants to know?"

"The Exterminator."

Robert extended his right hand to shake the Exterminator's as he believed using the left hand to be sacrilegious and because it hurt wearing the cumbersome leather gloves. "I hear you're interested in joining the cause?"

"Very much so."

"Good. Let's talk further, but not here. There's a bench located in the centre of the park."

Both men headed for the park's centre. Along the way, they discussed various ideologies and strategies on how to defeat their enemies. Basically, anything they didn't agree with, they knocked down through unintelligent conversation.

"Come here around ten o'clock tonight. I want to see you demonstrate these skills you claim to possess," said Robert.

The Exterminator nodded. "I certainly will just do that, and you will find that you won't be disappointed."

Night fell across Cleveland, and it was raining softly on this autumn evening. Robert's station wagon pulled up at the same place as this morning, near the park's entrance. He waited in his car for his newfound younger disciple, whom he only knew as the Exterminator. He grew impatient because the Exterminator was late by forty minutes and pondered whether this was all some kind of ruse. The thought of being set up by a vigilante group crossed his mind. He was about to utter profanity when he heard a strong knock on his car window.

"Leader, my apologies for being late. My girlfriend was being difficult. It won't happen again."

"It better not, because I was beginning to worry."

The Exterminator got into Robert's car, and they waited. They waited for some unsuspecting victim who didn't look like them. And they waited rather impatiently until two young men kissed each other lovingly under a nearby tree. As Robert and the Exterminator watched them with venomous revulsion, they got out of the station wagon. The Exterminator was carrying a flick knife, and they proceeded towards their prey.

The Exterminator took the young couple by surprise and began beating them ruthlessly while at the same time yelling profanities at them. Robert looked on, cowardly and gladly thinking, why should they have it so easy? While watching, he slightly touched his concealed deformity on his left hand. Then the Exterminator pulled his flick knife open and was about to cut the face of one of the young men when they heard Robert yelling at him to stop as he had just heard a police car's siren. Robert was secretly relieved, and the Exterminator fled the scene. The two young men left there tried to get up to reach the police and heard Robert and his thuggish new pal drive off, leaving them to come to terms with this brutal attack.

In Robert's car as he drove away cowardly, he quickly grew irritated by the Exterminator's laughter. "Will you just shut up! We failed!"

"But we sure let them queers know a thing or two."

"That may be so, but I have a more crucial, strategic target in mind."

"What?"

"Not what. Who. A Black evangelist called Brooks."

"Theodore Brooks?"

"Yeah."

"Are you nuts? He's well protected. We won't get anywhere close to him."

Robert didn't like the sound of the so-called Exterminator's tone suddenly and was becoming peeved with him. "I've a plan. If you feel you're not up to eliminating a pivotal figure in African American culture, then get out now."

The Exterminator paused for a moment. "I never said that I'm not in. We have to plan this meticulously if we have a hope in hell of succeeding, that's all."

"You let me worry about that."

Robert proceeded to drop the Exterminator home and headed back to his own house. When he got there, he had a warm shower, an act that to him washed away any negativity and not sin as others would describe it. After all, he didn't believe the nefarious acts that he had carried out this evening were in any way evil. He then cooked himself a nice steak meal and got a bottle of Scotch from underneath the TV and sat back on his armchair, imbibing. He fell asleep.

He felt wheezy, and things for a moment were surreal. It was as if he was dreaming. He was dreaming. Again, the dreaming experience was lucid. He was back in his tidy house, the exact same one as in his first dream featuring that place the night before. It seemed to be morning, and the doorbell chimed. He forced himself to find out who it could be as he was in a very disorientated state. He opened the door, and there to his wistful shock and surprise was, in the flesh, Theodore Brooks greeting him with a warm smile. "Rob, it's so nice to see you again. I decided to take you up on your warm and very kind invitation to come to your home."

Robert screamed! And awoke. His head was throbbing with a pounding headache. He looked around his home. Everything was normal in the sense that his house was an untidy dump. He checked the front door, opened it, and discovered that nobody was there.

"So, this is how it all begins," he said to himself. His thoughts meandered from thinking it was all down to a guilty conscience or the man above punishing him for his misdeeds. This, however, seemed to contradict his entire personal belief system, which was now becoming a major conflict in his mind. Deep down, he had no regrets about what he did as he believed himself to be right, but what else was it? This ever-current annoying thought sweeping his mind was beginning to plague his entire psyche.

He got on with his day, carrying out the same mundane duties as yesterday and the days before. It was time for his next radio broadcast. Because of his increasing angst, all neurotransmitter synapses at once became problematic for him. As he had no new material prepared due to the previous night's activities, he decided to diverge from his standard program format and try a listener call-in show for a few hours.

CHAPTER
THREE

After a useless radio phone-in show where nothing intelligent was said, Robert Emerson now knew that if ever he was going to achieve his life's goal, then now was the time. He had obtained the home address of Theodore Brooks from one of his operatives recently. He called up the Exterminator and told him today was the fateful day to teach him a valuable lesson, thus hopefully removing him as a threat to reform young black men from a life of crime. Robert believed that these young men were incapable of reforming, that they were indeed all malignant and spread their malignancy across America because he believed God created them solely to be subservient to the white race.

The Exterminator arrived at this poor, unfortunate, emotionally retarded idiot's home—that was Robert Emerson's house—and of course, he let him in, only to be eager to hand over his detailed plans unashamedly to him. He made sure he had his black leather gloves on to prevent the Exterminator from seeing any abnormality and to stop him from perceiving him as a weaker individual. When the Exterminator asked who would deal with Brooks, Robert sighed, "I will, of course."

They packed their Neo-Nazi gear and a loaded shotgun as they were heading to Brooks' home. The Exterminator couldn't help but notice how superfluous his role was in the assassination. He had been told by Robert that he was the driver, to drive them off after the hit. On their journey to Brooks' home, they were each silent. They had in common a few things, such as not discussing their intended goal in conversation, fearing in some way one of them would jeopardise their luck. Neo-Nazis, especially those two, were very superstitious and extremely cautious. They believed their cause was righteous despite the obvious biblical contradictions to their own precepts. They were as regressive as they were because they hated progress in technologies and political policies regarding multiculturalism, as this eroded their future functions, fearing that their kind would become obsolete. And that's why they set out at every endeavour to impede these kinds of progress, which Theodore Brooks was the actual personification of.

It was late afternoon now, and Robert knew from the intel that he had acquired that Brooks would be arriving home from his office any second now. And that fateful moment arrived as Brooks drove along into the cul-de-sac where his house was situated. He didn't suspect anything as Robert and the Exterminator were parked across the street. Brooks blessed himself with a ritual he always undertook before he would enter or exit his car. He got out, and as he was doing so, the Exterminator crept up behind him like a sly snake and fired the shotgun. Brooks fell to the ground. He was shot in the back, and the bullet hit his heart, killing him stone dead. Robert stared at him in deep shock. He couldn't believe the Exterminator had just ended his life. He heard the Exterminator yelling at him and ran back to the getaway car.

Brooks' wife and two teenage daughters rushed out from their house after hearing the shotgun discharge. They watched as the two thugs sped off. His wife ran over to her husband's body to discover this terrible truth. She became distraught. Her two daughters tried to comfort her but were unable to carry out this task as they too were in shock and consumed with grief.

In the getaway car, the Exterminator squealed with childish laughter. Robert told him to shut up, and as he stared into space, he could not begin to curb the deadly tension that was forming in his stomach and beginning to clench his heart. That night, after witnessing the Exterminator drinking himself sick in a secluded quarry on the outskirts of Cleveland, Robert, who was imbibing Scotch, yelled at him, "You idiot! Why did you have to murder him?"

"I did it because you were too cowardly to do it yourself!"

"I only wanted to teach him a lesson, just to get him afraid."

"You were unable to do it, so I stepped in and saved you the bother. You should thank me."

Robert wanted to be away from him. Even amid his drunken stupor, he wanted to dream. Dreaming, he perceived, would be the only escape from his feelings of deep guilt that he was now experiencing for aiding and abetting in the taking of Theodore Brooks' life.

He lay supine on the damp grass, but he didn't care as he stared up at the anomaly of the Betelgeuse nova. He couldn't keep his eyes open anymore, and Robert drifted off into a deep sleep. In his dream, he was standing in front of Brooks. Brooks smiled at him and said, "The invitation that you were very kind to issue, Rob, remember?"

"Come inside," he muttered in response.

Brooks obeyed his instruction and entered. "My wife

couldn't make it. She is extremely busy these days at the church."

"Please take a seat."

"Thank you, Rob."

Brooks sat down. Robert's head was swirling with anxiety. "Why are you really here?"

"Isn't it obvious? As I said, your kind invite."

"How could you be here now?"

Brooks thought for a second. He saw that the man asking him this question was clearly confused. "Rob, are you alright?"

"Of course I'm alright! And I know for a fact that I would never invite someone like you to my home," Robert said angrily. He stood up, about to gesture to his unwanted guest to leave, when Brooks stood up too and read him the riot act. "Excuse me?! You mean that your invitation to your home was a ploy to educate me on how you really feel about people like me, people who share the same colour skin as me?"

Robert smirked. "I just believe that black is black and white is white, for a good, fundamental reason, that's all."

Brooks was surprised but not completely shocked. He was used to white people who pretended to accept him, only deep down he really knew what they thought. "And what would that reason be?"

"God's," Robert yelled at him in his face. "Black embodies all things dark and evil."

Brooks was trying hard to prevent himself from becoming totally irate. He shook his head and replied despondently back to Robert. "As if there aren't any white folks carrying out the devil's work."

Brooks turned around and headed to his car. As he made his way, he turned back to Robert and said with a strong tone that emboldened grave disappointment at what he had just heard, "You know, Robert, the Bible says God loves all, everybody, regardless. You're just another prejudiced person who doesn't understand why his hatred is contradictory. Your beliefs cancel out each other. You're nothing but a Jesus-hating bastard!"

Robert's veins filled with fury, and he charged at Brooks as he made his way to the car, only he awoke screaming. "I am deranged. I wish I could take it off my head and throw it away, far from my mind. Damn! What crap am I saying?"

Robert returned home the next morning. He hurried to the kitchen and poured himself a glass of water. He was beginning to suffer the onset of a pounding headache. Realising he needed a distraction, he switched on the radio. There was a guest speaker on a talk show discussing the detrimental effects of the Betelgeuse nova. He was called Professor Edgar Sloane, and much to the incredulous nature of the host, it was what he said next on air that rattled Robert off his axis.

"There is someone in Cleveland, Ohio who is undergoing the said effects directly. The fate of the universe is at stake, and it's all down to the anomaly in space. You see, when the Betelgeuse nova occurred, it created a shockwave at the subatomic level which copied our planet and solar system and shoved this copy into a quantum pocket, thus duplicating matter and biological life."

The radio host was incredulous at what this Sloane was saying. "You mean to say that over sixty years ago everybody on Earth was copied, and these copies of us now exist in a micro universe?"

"Yes, that's exactly what I'm saying."

"Does this quantum micro universe still exist?"

Sloane cleared his throat. "Oh, yes, only people living there today wouldn't be strictly carbon copies. Six decades is a long time, and our macro universe as well as the micro universe have taken different paths—all down to free will. That's why it's imperative that I find someone, as I need to speak to him at once," Sloane warned.

The radio host wasn't buying any of this and was told in her ear to end the interview by her producers. Robert realised he had to find this Edgar Sloane and meet him at once; otherwise, these peculiar dreams would never cease.

CHAPTER
FOUR

Edgar Sloane became irritated over the radio host suddenly discontinuing his call. He hated being perceived as a "prank" and wanted desperately to find whoever was imminently going to cause massive cosmic chaos. He thought about going on social media and considered it when the phone rang. He didn't recognise the number but answered it. "Yes?"

"Are you him?" the male voice asked.

"Are you Sloane?"

"The answer to your question depends on who's asking."

"I've been having these crazy dreams where I'm in the life of some alternate version of myself, only I'm the complete opposite to the person I truly am. Does that make any sense to you, Sloane?"

"Just who are you?" asked Sloane.

"I'm Robert Emerson, and I need your help to stop me from losing my mind."

"Where are you now?"

"Cleveland, Ohio."

"Don't go anywhere, Mister Emerson. I'm about five hundred miles from there. I'll get the next train to your city and book a hotel. Contact me on this number at this time tomorrow."

"Please tell me what's going on with me here?"

"Tomorrow. I'll be able to shed some light on your predicament. Hold still till then."

Robert put down the phone. He realised that Sloane might not be the phoney that he first thought he was and waited. The day passed, and Robert's anxiety levels increased much to his distress. He went to bed late but failed to dream vividly like before, much to his badly needed peace of mind. It was the next morning, and he arose early from bed. He showered and shaved and put on his best suit. He wanted desperately to conceal his true personality and profession from this Edgar Sloane.

Robert waited rather nervously for the time to call back Sloane's cellphone. It was five minutes away from the desired time. He pondered how he was going to stop himself from flying off the handle if Sloane said anything invidious regarding references to a better left-wing governed state. He always feared this facet of his dark, troubled personality. The five minutes were up, and he quickly called Sloane. "Sloane, are you in Cleveland yet?"

Sloane coughed a dry cough. "Yes, find me in the Grande Hotel. It's on..."

"I know where that dump is. I'll be there in an hour."

Robert realised Sloane was probably a trickster if he was staying in a shithole like the Grande Hotel. But what choice had he got? He got into his jeep and headed to just outside the downtown area of Cleveland. The traffic was light, much to his surprise. When he arrived, he got out of his jeep and headed steadily to the Grande Hotel's foyer. Once inside, he gazed around the room. There were middle-aged to old-aged married couples having drinks. "Where is he?" he asked himself.

Then he heard a dry cough from a man. It sounded like Sloane's dry cough on the phone. He turned his head in the direction of this man coughing and saw a tall, thin man with grey hair and a moustache drinking a scotch. Robert approached this strange-looking man. He whispered lightly to him, "Are you Sloane?"

The man nodded his head. "Emerson, right?"

"Yep, that's me, and let me tell you from the word go that if you're fucking with me, then I'll make you very sorry. Just tell me what's going on with me."

"It's got to do with what's going on up in the sky."

"You mean that damned star that exploded decades ago?"

Sloane coughed again. "Yes, the Betelgeuse nova. It has created an anomaly that is affecting space and time. In your dreams, you are in the mind of your alternate self from the micro universe. I believe you're the key to preventing a major catastrophe from taking place, Mister Emerson."

Robert became suddenly taken aback and astonished. He was not having any of this. He grabbed Sloane by the neck and, grinding his teeth, spoke, "Listen here, you quack. You mean to tell me that I'm going to be the cause of ending the world? It's people like you, fucking libertarians, that's ending everything as we once knew it! Why don't you go back to whatever queerish rock you crawled out from under."

He stopped holding Sloane's neck and gave him a chance to breathe. "You dumb bastard, Emerson. I never said that you were the cause, only that you are in fact the cure."

Robert rolled his eyes. "Damn you anyway. Tell me what's really going on."

Sloane became seated once again, swallowed the remaining scotch, and looked Robert Emerson straight in the eyes and told him firmly, "For some unknown reason which I've yet to solve, and the fact that I've been receiving messages on my computer system which also shouldn't be happening, I have been informed you, and indeed you are the key to solving all these quandaries. You must join me in an isolated cave where we have both been instructed to go."

"What cave, and where in the hell is it?"

"It's located in the Jornada del Muerto Desert down in New Mexico," replied Sloane, still unsure whether Robert was taking this in.

"When do we leave?"

"I've all the needs and means of transportation organised. It will be the day after tomorrow. I'll be in touch."

Sloane got up and headed to the elevator to take him to his room. Robert figured that he and everything he was talking about had tired him out. He himself left the hotel, and on his way to his jeep, something came into his mind. He had to see someone first before he went gallivanting off to New Mexico with Sloane. He drove to a small town located ten miles from Cleveland. He arrived at a church. This was the home of the Reverend Verne Carlisle.

Robert proceeded to the front door of the house and rang the doorbell. It opened, and to his relief, it was him. "Robert, great to see you again! What brings you all the way out here?"

"Verne, I am very troubled. I really need to see you, if possible."

"Please, Robert. Join me in my home."

Inside the Reverend Carlisle's house were nice furniture neatly arranged, and everything was tidy. There was a large metal Latin cross in the centre of the room where both men became seated nearby. The Reverend's wife came in with coffee and biscuits. Robert felt uneasy and declined. She excused herself and went into another room, closing the door after her.

Reverend Carlisle knew how distraught Robert was feeling just by looking at him. He spoke to him softly and asked, "Robert, confide in me. You can trust me."

Robert became reluctant to speak but couldn't hold back anymore. He needed to be heard. "Ever since I began hating and blaming the establishment in all its forms and those who represent and support it, I just want to bring them all down with me because I have nothing."

"God has a plan for you, Robert and he will in some way find a way to assuage your pain."

"Now, you're beginning to sound like Sloane, and I know he's one crazy bastard. Will you kindly tell me just what it is that you all require from me."

"You, Robert. I strongly believe that you have been blessed with a miraculous gift. I'm not fully sure what it is or what you have to do with it, but there will come a time where everything will fall into place. Then you will have all your questions answered."

Tears descended from Robert's stony eyes. This was followed by the inevitable surge of guilt that he had been repressing for days now. He turned to the Reverend and spoke softly. "Verne, I helped kill a man just a few days ago. I didn't want it that way, but I'm not sure if I am sorry or if I now have the need to confide in someone like you."

The Reverend Carlisle was shocked and felt as if he had just been hit by a catapult. He sighed because, after all, he knew only too well that Robert was a dark man. So, he decided not to respond with words, only just simpering a dead smile. Robert knew that was his cue to leave. He got up and left the house. As he made his way to his jeep, he could not help but wonder if the Reverend was going to dob him in, for now, he didn't care much about things. His cellphone rang from his seat in the jeep. He realised that he had forgotten to bring it inside with him. He opened the door and picked it up. It was Sloane.

Sloane was angry and sounded very much so. "Emerson, I've been ringing you all afternoon. I had to bring things forward by a few days."

"Okay, Sloane, I hear you. I'll meet you back at the Grande Hotel tonight. The sooner I get away from all of this, the better."

With that said, Robert checked into the Grande Hotel himself. As he was heading to his room, he met Sloane in the corridor. He was carrying a bottle in a brown bag. Sloane signalled to Robert to join him for a nightcap, and that's exactly what they did. Almost all the cheap bottle of whiskey which Sloane had bought was now imbibed by the two men. They were both very much inebriated now and started revealing personal insights to each other without any qualms. Sloane reached out for the bottle, but Robert grabbed it back off him. "It's mine, dammit!" he said as he took another slug from it.

"OK! Good job I'm not your wife."

Robert sniggered. "I am not married, and I guess never will be."

"Why not?" asked Sloane.

"Why not? Eh? That's a good question, I guess. I suppose women I don't get. I don't even register with their perception of me. Sure, I had a few chances with some of them, but they—"

Robert muttered, extending his left arm and displaying to Sloane his handicap.

"I think I understand," replied Sloane with a sympathetic touch.

"They see something in me that turns them right off me.

I'm no freak, maybe a hateful bastard, and they detect my rage."

"Women and people in general think this rage defines you?"

"Probably. Of course, I'm angry! I've been rejected and ostracised! All because I have one arm shorter than the other! You know, sometimes I really despise women. It's like their feminine instincts never switch off, and I'm therefore automatically eliminated from their selection process," replied Robert as he flung the now empty bottle of scotch across the room, just missing Sloane's head.

"Watch it! Damn you!" Sloane said because he was startled. He knew there was great pain to Robert's words as he spoke them. This, he realised, couldn't have been easy for him to bring to the surface. He stared into Robert's eyes and began to speak solemn words to him, "Robert, what you have just revealed to me affirms how right I am about you and bringing you on this special journey."

"How so?" uttered Robert as he burped.

"I can see you have the rare ability to look into yourself so deeply. Your personal insights, I imagine, will prove invaluable on your mission."

Robert felt drowsy, and his head was aching. It was too long of a journey to drive to the suburbs, so he decided to stay. He went into his room and lay on the made bed, staring up at the ceiling, pondering how all of this ever happened to him and why. Conversations with Reverend Carlisle and Sloane filled his troubled mind. They each had their similarities and contradictions. Deciding all this mental mayhem was becoming too much for him, he closed his eyes and fell asleep.

The next thing, he was dreaming, and this meant that he was back in the micro universe, back in the alternate version of his house. He was in bed, naked under the sheets, when a scantily dressed Asian girl in red lingerie walked into his bedroom, smiling. It was Jessica. He tried to cover up his left hand and noticed a wedding ring on his finger. She had one too. They were married in this reality. The shock of this surged through his soul. Thoughts of how a beautiful woman like Jessica could have accepted him enough to have him as her husband, which was something he had been searching for his entire life. Suddenly, he didn't care about her race. He instantly awoke, and he was back in his room at the Grande Hotel. He was speechless because his mind was telling him to have revulsion at such a circumstance; however, his body and heart told him, and made him, highly aroused, and he experienced feelings of happiness. He wanted to go back there desperately to be with her.

CHAPTER
FIVE

Back at the Grande Hotel, Sloane frantically packed his suitcase. He was nervous and becoming increasingly irritable over Robert being late. These miserable thoughts were interrupted when Robert opened his room door. "Are we ready to head?" Robert asked.

"I thought I locked that bloody thing. Anyone could come in. I'm becoming careless," Sloane replied.

"Will you stop fretting and get us there already!"

"I'm all packed and we're ready to go. Have you got all that you need?"

"Yeah, I'm ready as I'll ever be," replied Robert.

Both Robert and Sloane left the Grande Hotel. Robert drove his station wagon out of Cleveland with his unusual passenger along for the journey to the Jornada del Muerto Desert in New Mexico, where Sloane had trains and buses all organised. He even had the phone numbers of cabs who could bring them as close as they could get to the cave—the all-important, pivotal cave that he raved about.

The two men appeared incongruent at the Amtrak station

in Cleveland. Sloane had the next train booked to take them all the way to Santa Fe Railyard in New Mexico, where they would get on a bus to bring them as near as possible to the desert, where Sloane had his equipment in the hidden cave. Robert felt somewhat embarrassed at being in Sloane's company for what would be an incredibly long journey. He pretended that he was travelling alone in case some of his colleagues saw him. God knew what conclusion they would form in their minds should they stumble upon Robert Emerson being pals with some weak weirdo like Sloane. He wasn't always this self-conscious, but being nervous and combining the obvious mistrust towards his travelling partner helped formulate these emotions on this afternoon.

After almost two weeks of bus and train switching, Sloane organised a cab carrying Robert and himself to a small, dusty town not far from the cave. This town, called Clayton, New Mexico, was a dump and there was nothing in it apart from some hapless hicks. They watched as Robert and Sloane got out of the cab, wondering what they were up to here in Clayton. Sloane warned in a whisper to ignore them, but Robert couldn't help but snarl at them to fend them off. Both men hadn't planned on availing themselves of this tiny hamlet's limited accommodations and instead were going to rough it nearby the location of the cave.

"How is that tent going to serve two of us?" asked Robert, a little concerned.

"Relax! I'm not intending to sleep beside you or anything remotely like that. The tent is for you and you alone. I intend to sleep staring up at the Anomaly. It always guarantees me a good night's dreams."

"Speaking of which, when are you going to knock me out so I can project my mind into my counterpart's?"

Sloane winced. "Not here. I'll put you out when you're

inside the cave. There I'll inject you with a concentrated dose of melatonin to knock you out for a few days, and when you appear to be awakening, I'll administer it again. And tomorrow morning, I will take you inside the cave and explain all to you."

Robert became a little worried. He had his guard fully up and wasn't going to allow Sloane to try anything funny. "Just be careful, Sloane. I may be out for the count but trust me, I'll be fully aware if you fuck with me."

"I'd expect nothing less of you. It will go as I say. Now get some *natural* sleep."

Robert didn't dream—or more to the point, didn't project his consciousness to that of his counterpart—instead, he couldn't remember if he dreamt at all during the night. He was feeling drowsy and was about to doze off again when he heard the strident banging of a wooden spoon beating against a saucepan. "Wake up!" Sloane shouted.

Robert flinched and yelled over to him, "What the hell's that racket for?"

Sloane stopped beating the wooden spoon against the saucepan and replied, "We haven't got all day!"

Robert sighed and asked himself, "Just what in the hell have I signed up for?"

Sloane dropped the saucepan and the wooden spoon after it, much to the irritation of Robert. "Can I ask you a question?" Sloane asked.

"What?!" replied Robert, angered.

"Why are you all the way out here?"

Robert grunted and stood up, catching Sloane by the neck and yelling into his face, "You'd better not have put me on some wild goose chase. I was dumb enough to follow you down here thinking that I was chosen for an important, eternal role, all because I let you think that I was experiencing an epiphany!"

Robert flung Sloane back on his arse, and he picked himself up from the dirt. "Please continue, answer my question," continued Sloane.

"I'm here for the white race! To prove that we are indeed superior because a man with my beliefs and convictions was especially chosen to embolden this fact," Robert responded, with a surge of hubristic pride coursing through his veins.

"It's funny. I've always endeavoured for a united world with one people to ensure a trouble-free society."

"Sloane, you lefty libertine! Don't you know that such a preposterous ideal like that could never work? There are just too many derivative differences, ideologies, and beliefs that would all conflict with one another. No, to truly make sure in avoiding conflict, you must keep the races separate. In that way, they can't interact with one another, thus avoiding contention. And the way to fix everything is to banish those immigrants back to where they came from and close the borders, or else strip them of certain rights and privileges, such as running for parliament and voting. The white man and woman are the most evolutionarily advanced forms of human being there is. The others came from the dirt and can return to the dirt for all I care," Robert said, without an ounce of humility or basic understanding.

Sloane just rolled his eyes. Somehow his mind had drifted away with the fairies as Robert was spouting that crap. He had never stumbled upon a fully-fledged right-wing activist like him before, and his beliefs were contrary to his own. He decided to lighten the tone and proceeded to prepare some refreshments. He set the small gas burner he had brought in his satchel and took out a jar of coffee. He, as opposed to Robert, was going to have a fruit tea.

"Does that answer your question?" asked Robert, smirking.

Sloane became puzzled. He didn't realise what Robert was

referring to, as he was much too bamboozled by what had just been yelled into his face. He had the spit from Robert's venomous yelling still on his cheeks. "I'm sorry, what question was that?"

"You asked me the fucking reason as to why I agreed to volunteer to go to the other side, to the micro universe, and take part in this highfalutin experiment of yours."

Sloane felt like an idiot. He was becoming nervous. "Oh, that question. How silly of me. Do you want some coffee?"

Robert nodded, and an awkward silence loomed in the air. Robert gazed upon the horizon and became quickly startled when he noticed a tall, strange-looking silhouette of somebody not too far away. Sloane was making noise preparing the coffee, and Robert exhorted, "Shush!"

"What?" Sloane asked.

"Are you sure nobody knows about this place?"

"Why?"

"We must've been followed. There's a weirdo nearby."

Robert moved closer to this person, but then he couldn't believe what he saw next. This person just vanished right before his eyes. "Did you see that?"

Sloane became annoyed. "Will you stop? I didn't see a thing."

But that wasn't good enough for Robert. He went over to his sports bag, took out and quickly assembled his rifle. He wasn't leaving anything to chance. Sloane poured him a warm tin mug of coffee and presented it to him. Robert snapped the mug out of his hands, scalding Sloane. "What's wrong with you?" he demanded.

"I told you to shut up. I'm going to do a perimeter sweep. This place must be made secure."

Sloane approached Robert and pulled him aside. He placed his right hand on Robert's left shoulder and spoke softly, "I think it's time we got ready. Your quest is about to begin."

Robert calmed down. He realised that if there was ever a faithful time to get on this quest, it was now. "Ok. Let's do it."

Sloane gestured to Robert to follow him about three hundred metres away from the campsite. They arrived at the cave soon after, and Robert was amazed at how a large arched rock stood over its entrance. Sloane took out a flashlight and handed it to Robert, then took another one for himself. They switched them both on and walked slowly inside through the cavern. Robert felt somewhat excited at the notion that he was about to be transported somewhere else, like the micro universe, and of course, seeing that reality's version of Jessica again.

Sloane arrived at a metal door. He urged Robert to be still as he took out his keys. He then proceeded to open this door to allow them both to go deeper inside the cavern. Robert stepped cautiously and slowly inside. He noticed a bed that was hooked up to machines and, at the opposite end, a computer workstation.

Robert suddenly became a little too, and rightfully more, cautious. "Just how in God's name is all this going to work?"

Sloane didn't reply to him then and there. Instead, he went over to a makeshift cupboard and took out a modified VR headset.

"Don't tell me you're gonna put that on my head?" Robert asked, worried.

"I have to," replied Sloane condescendingly. "It's used to stimulate your neurotransmitter activity and match your brain's electrical synapses to the frequencies generated by the energy field of the Anomaly."

"You're gonna end up killing me!" Robert said wistfully to himself.

Sloane laughed. "No, not at all. All that you see here is designed to bring you on your journey safely."

"How do you know all this? What possessed you with this special knowledge to achieve this?"

Sloane walked slowly over to his computer workstation and booted the system up. He then opened a program and began explaining it to Robert. "This computer program that I'm showing you was designed by myself using Artificial Intelligence. AI helps me come up with this 'special knowledge', and I can safely argue that you're in safe hands, Robert."

"I guess it's now or never, then."

"Yes, I guess it is. Are you ready, Robert?"

Robert nodded. Sloane gestured to him to take off his clothes and slip into sleepwear while he turned away to afford him privacy. As Robert got into the bed, he pondered for a moment about expressing some more doubts, but then realised he would only be wasting more time. Sloane attached electrodes to his forehead and throughout his body so he could monitor his subject's vitals. He then picked up the headset and moved closer over to Robert, who was now lying in the bed staring up at the cave's ceiling.

As Sloane fixed the headset onto Robert's head carefully, he urged him to begin counting the cobwebs on the ceiling. He then picked up a vial containing a purple substance and intravenously administered a strong sedative to him. Robert flinched, and then his vision blurred as he tried to count the cobwebs. Then that was it. He was out cold.

Sloane ran immediately over to his workstation and switched on the headset. He turned back over and saw Robert in a deep sleep. "Godspeed and good luck!"

CHAPTER SIX

Robert opened his eyes and stared at the ceiling of a living room that was vaguely familiar and soon realised that Sloane had been successful in transporting his consciousness into his counterpart's body in the micro-universe. He quickly discovered that his head was aching, and he was lying on the floor. He tried to get up—it was a struggle, but he managed it. He looked around and remembered that he had seen this place before in his dreams, and now he was here with a sense of control and understanding.

He rubbed his head and noticed he was bruised a little, but this didn't prevent him from investigating things here. As he got himself to stand upright, something immediately struck him dumbfounded: a framed picture of himself, his wife, Jessica, and their teenage daughter, all happily together for a family photograph. He felt his wedding band on the fourth finger of his left hand, which was still in the same condition as when he was born. He moved closer to it and picked it up from the mantelpiece. He stared at it for a few moments and pondered that this version of Robert Emerson, or "Rob" as he was called, was a blessed man. Blessed for having such a beautiful wife and daughter, and for having a self-assuring and loving foundation in his formative years to enable him to possess such happiness.

Robert's reverie was quickly disrupted when he heard the upstairs door open. He was startled somewhat and heard footsteps coming down the stairs. Again, he was dumbstruck. This person was his alternate's daughter, *his* daughter in the micro-universe.

"Dad, have you seen my iPad?" she asked.

"Ahh…" Robert muttered. He knew what an iPad was but obviously hadn't come across one yet. "Ah, no. I haven't."

"Did you fall?" she asked, genuinely concerned.

He was pleasantly surprised by how delightful she sounded, as well as by how caring she was. Then her phone rang with a sweet-sounding tone.

"It's Mom," she said, as she pressed a button to answer the call.

"Angelica, I'm still waiting!" Jessica's voice said on the other end.

"Where's your mother now, *Angelica?*" asked Robert.

"She's outside, waiting in her car. I'd better be going—I'm already late for school."

Angelica kissed Robert on the cheek and followed that with a warm hug. "Catch you later, Dad."

For the first time since he was a child, Robert felt naturally pleasant, good feelings swimming through his veins. He was happy.

Angelica headed out the door to meet her mother, who was waiting impatiently for her. Robert sat down on the sofa and smiled to himself. This feeling of greatness was shattered when he remembered that his newfound family could be inconsequential to the reasons as to why he really was sent on this journey in the first place. He got up and decided to investigate the world around him. He thought that family photo albums would be a good place to begin, so he began searching the cupboards. But first, how could he have forgotten to do the most primary thing since he arrived here? He stepped outside —the neighbourhood looked much like his own—and looked up and saw no evidence of the Anomaly in the sky. It simply wasn't there.

Robert also remembered that during the times when his consciousness was first being projected into this reality, he had encountered this reality's version of Theodore Brooks and had a quite distasteful confrontation with him. "Now, how am I going to explain this?" he thought. This was something he soon realised that he had overlooked and was unprepared for. After all, Brooks could call at this house again, and he would be done for. He decided to put this matter on the back burner for now and saw Jessica arriving home. As she drove her car into the driveway, his nerves were in turmoil. Jessica got out of the car and walked over to her husband. She kissed him on the lips, and there was no denying that it felt so nice.

"I must go into town. Remember, you said you'd help me pick out a suite of furniture for the living room?"

Robert struggled for a moment. Of course, he couldn't recall anything like that. "Oh, yes," he muttered.

"You don't remember our conversation at all, do you, Rob?"

Robert thought fast but still couldn't come up with any excuse.

Jessica smiled. "That's ok. I suppose it's because the Reverend Brooks is calling in under an hour?"

"What?!" Robert exclaimed.

Jessica giggled. "Don't worry. I'm sure he will be his plain, pleasant self as always. How are the blackouts?"

Robert didn't know what she was referring to. "All better now."

"I've got to shower. Let me know when we can go into town."

She made her way into the bathroom. Robert was worried. Soon Brooks would be arriving, and this wasn't going to be easy.

Robert waited and waited for his visitation from Theodore Brooks. All kinds of things were flooding through his mind. The fact that he had allowed and couldn't prevent his "real" counterpart from being slain by the Exterminator, and the insults he had traded with him during his brief projection to this reality not that long ago.

The doorbell rang stridently and startled him. He took in a deep breath and answered it. To his unsurprise, it was indeed Brooks on the other side, looking quite stern.

"Emerson, I want you to know that I am banning you from the church. Your family are still welcome, but I don't want to see you anywhere near it," Brooks said.

"Listen, Reverend, I can explain."

"Explain that you're a racist? You made your views pretty clear a few weeks ago. Stay away from me!"

Robert now realised something strategic that he had to do. No matter what his personal views on Brooks in the prime reality, he couldn't afford to display them to the man in front of him now roaring at him. "I can help make things better for the church."

Brooks became infuriated. Because he had no idea of Robert's real motives regarding this situation, he just saw red. "Remember the Holocaust? Remember how the Nazis, with whom you profess to share beliefs, rounded up small children, took them from their crying mothers? And how these children were oblivious to chambers of fire where they were burned alive—that's only one of the sadistic deeds they carried out. How would you like it if Angelica were one of them?"

An icy shiver ran down Robert's spine, and he turned white as a ghost. That mere thought condemned him to a cold hell should such a scenario ever be realised. He couldn't answer him. So, Brooks turned around and headed to his car. Robert shut the door and waited for Jessica to come back out from the bathroom.

Shame and this type of fear were feelings he was unfamiliar with in this context, and they were something Robert was now experiencing. He tried to dismiss them, as he did when he heard such arguments in the past, only this time it was different—he had a daughter. He went back inside and closed the door. He sat down and thought simply as an indulging distraction: what if his counterpart's mind make-up differed from his own, not to mention his entire personality? He found himself unable to switch off the autonomically produced emotional reactions that conflicted directly with this version of himself's internal personal core belief system.

Jessica had finished her shower and was blow-drying her hair. She hadn't heard the discourse between her husband and Brooks. She came down the stairs. "All go well with him?" she asked.

Robert was clearly not used to this kind of domesticity and was gauche in his mannerisms toward her. All he could reply was, "I don't feel too well. I'm afraid I can't go into town with you today."

"It's the blackouts, isn't it?"

"Yes."

"That's it. I'm calling Doctor Carlisle."

"Carlisle? Verne Carlisle?"

"Yes, him. This's worse than I thought. Where's my iPhone?"

She noticed where her phone was as quickly as she asked him. "Oh, it's there." She picked it up and proceeded to call him.

Robert felt extremely confused. He hadn't a clue what was going on. "Really, I'm fine," he spoke.

"I'm not taking any chances. You're seeing him and that's final."

What could Robert do but decide to play along? So he acquiesced, and she drove him to Doctor Carlisle's general practice.

As Robert, who was in the passenger seat, watched the world of the micro-universe—or more specifically the alternate city of Cleveland—he couldn't help but notice how it was virtually the same except for a small number of subtle nuisances, which slightly irked him.

"We're here," said Jessica. "Let me help you out of the car."

"It's ok. I'm ok—I can manage."

Jessica ignored his plea of stubbornness and helped him anyway.

They walked slowly up the steps to the practice. Once inside, they noticed the waiting room was empty. This meant he could be seen almost straight away.

Jessica notified the receptionist, and she buzzed Carlisle. Robert, escorted by his wife, went into the doctor's office.

"Doctor Carlisle, my husband has been experiencing blackouts for the last number of weeks. Once, I found him at the doorstep unconscious."

"How long was he out for?"

"I'm not sure how long."

Robert was getting pissed off, so he interjected as quickly as he could, "Listen, Reverend, I'm really fine now."

"*Reverend*? I'm not a religious man, nor will I ever be. This must be more serious than I suspected."

"How could I be so dumb?" Robert thought. He knew things were slightly upside down in this reality. "Sorry, I was thinking of someone else."

Carlisle cleared his throat with a loud, dry cough. "I think I should send you to get checked out. I think it's only prudent, given the circumstances."

"Sure, when?" asked Jessica.

"I'll arrange an MRI for tomorrow afternoon."

Robert realised that he was beaten. Arguing with them, he knew, was futile, so he nodded his head in agreement. After all, what's the worst that could happen? Right?

Jessica drove him back home. To say that Robert was experiencing some kind of derealised state was an understatement. On the one hand, he had a beautiful wife and daughter, and on the other, he was someone who was held in high esteem in this reality.

That night, after his wife made him a nice supper and poured him a glass of warm milk to help him sleep, Robert counted his lucky stars. And then, out of nowhere, a thought pondered through his mind: the Betelgeuse star—it never went nova here, and he wondered why.

CHAPTER
SEVEN

Robert had a peaceful night's sleep. He wondered how his physical body was doing back in the cave with Sloane monitoring him and all that life support nonsense that only that crazy scientist could manage. He also knew that Sloane could pull the plug on his body in the real world at any time, and if something pivotal was going to happen here, it ought to be soon.

Today was the day of his MRI scan, and he dreaded it. It was getting in his way and wasting time. He thought he'd better go through the motions with it, nonetheless. Once again, he got dressed, and Jessica drove him to the hospital. He didn't have to wait long, which was unusual for him because in his old life he didn't have adequate healthcare. He decided he wouldn't be stubborn, allowed the professionals to be professionals, and got on with it. He quickly noticed it would be a Middle Eastern doctor who would be carrying out his MRI, and his head hurt as before with the onset of a possible conflict in his mind regarding this man's race, so he stared in the opposite direction of him while he was speaking, watching a picture of a green bird. This annoyed the doctor, and he raised his voice sharply, telling Robert to listen to the instructions regarding the procedure.

The doctor placed the headset on Robert and carried out the scans on his brain. He grew perplexed at the readings. As Robert drifted away from that deafening, loud thumping sound, he saw Sloane's face, and he was laughing hideously. Then that face turned into the figure he had seen near the cave back in New Mexico when Sloane was arguing with him. This figure came closer and closer until he saw it was not a human being but a thing with a tall body and a large head, and it had two large black eyes and a short mouth. He screamed and realised he should push the emergency button. Afterwards, when Robert and Jessica were seated in the doctor's office waiting for the results, Robert couldn't get the image of the alien out of his mind.

That night, Jessica prepared a romantic meal for the both of them. She told him Angelica was spending the night at one of her friend's houses. She had champagne ready and waiting for them, all set out on a red tablecloth on a small table that signified intimacy and exclusivity. When Robert came down the stairs after a short snooze from the grueling MRI scans, he couldn't help but notice what a welcoming distraction the laid-out table was to the image of the alien in his mind. He felt he was becoming nervous about where the night was going to lead and because he hadn't ever been with a woman intimately before, all kinds of concerns arose.

"Happy anniversary, darling!" Jessica said, smiling as she proceeded to pour him a glass of champagne.

He had no idea that it was their wedding anniversary and immediately thought, Has this significance?

Robert became seated opposite his wife in this micro-universe reality, and she moved her hand amorously to his left hand, touching the wedding ring on his finger. Unsure whether to feel accepted or repulsed by himself, he didn't know. He reached out for the glass and swallowed a large amount of champagne. "Angelica is in Stacy's house tonight," he mused.

"I know. This is our special time. It has been seventeen years."

"Seventeen years!" Robert exclaimed aloud. "Oh, it went so fast," he continued, trying not to make things obvious.

"And it has been worth every day of it. I want you to know, Robert, how you took all the loneliness from my heart. Being a second-generation Chinese immigrant, it wasn't easy. Most of all, thank you for the beautiful gift of our daughter. Angelica is such a kind, sweet girl," Jessica said as she kissed him warmly on his lips.

Robert felt warm. Nice, pleasant feelings shrouded his once-tortured soul, and his heart felt enormous. He fell in love with the woman that he was supposed to be in love with in this reality. He dared not reveal his true life or his place in the world. Then sadness crept up his mind like a creepy, unsettling insect crawling along his back. He would have to leave her and Angelica once he had completed his mission here, whatever that was. But for now, he decided to enjoy this unique time in his life. That night, this couple, who were strongly in love, consummated this love. For Robert, it was the first time a woman accepted him and allowed him to express this mutual acceptance and love.

The next morning, Jessica was up early. She was deeply worried as Angelica hadn't arrived back from her friend's house. She called Stacy's parents, and Stacy's mother informed her that Angelica had never spent the night in their home. Jessica screamed and woke up Robert. He quickly ran down the stairs to find out what was happening.

"She's missing!" screamed Jessica to Robert.

"We'll find her, darling. Call the police and I'll call the school."

After much investigating, Angelica was nowhere to be found. Stacy told her parents and which in turn told Robert that she hadn't seen her since the end of the school day. Stacy also revealed that poor Angelica experienced bullying that day at school from some of the white boys. This was a watershed moment for him. Something he once condoned and practiced was now happening to his beloved daughter. He felt ashamed of himself for his past misdeeds and to all the victims where he inflicted this same kind of treatment on. Something struck him that he should get into his car and drive around the vicinity in searching for her. He assumed the rules of the road were exactly the same in the micro universe as back in his. He went over to the cupboard where he saw a bunch of keys that Jessica had left there only yesterday and assumed all the car keys were in the same place. He grabbed the ones that had the same emblem as the car in the garage. Jessica was still on the phone calling up every friend and mere acquaintance that their daughter had.

Robert stepped outside to find it was heavily raining. He hadn't wore his jacket and got soaked wet. He headed over to the garage and opened it. When he turned on the light, he became numb. Frozen with the shock of seeing Angelica hanging from the ceiling from a light beam where she used a rope. Tears descended from his stony eyes and now felt increasingly jaded in his soul. He could utter a cry or speak but managed to slightly pull himself together enough to go over to her to cut her down. As he moved closer to her body he could see something was written on her forehead with a felt marker. The word inscribed said, "unclean."

As he tried to take his newfound beloved daughter into his

arms he could see that she had been sexually violated. He became outraged and screamed, "Nooooh!"

Jessica heard her husband screaming from the kitchen and ran out to the garage. When she got inside she saw Robert carrying their dead daughter out to the house. She was frozen; in the horrible moment that was and with shock, disdain and grief. "Oh, my poor baby," she cried softly.

Robert couldn't help but feel extremely saddened for her and tried to console her by extending his hand. She embraced him and Angelica. "Why? How could this happen?" she asked, incredulously.

"I don't know, darling but I'm going to find out."

One thing for certain for Robert was the need to get revenge. He wasted no time in asking around regarding what happened. He was a teacher in the micro universe but not at Angelica's school. His school was the other side of Cleveland. He called up Angelica's school and one of the teachers told him that a kid named Billy McIntyre had been giving her a hard time over the past few weeks. This kid had been expelled for bullying other kids that weren't white and wasn't in school that day. This teacher also told Robert that other kids saw McIntyre follow Angelica home yesterday.

CHAPTER
EIGHT

Jessica put down the phone. She was very sombre, and as Robert approached her, she couldn't utter any words, just wiping the silent tears from her eyes with her hand. He felt helpless. He realised she had been speaking to Reverend Brooks to finalise Angelica's funeral arrangements. He hadn't done anything so far regarding Billy McIntyre and experienced a conflict in his head. His mind was at war. On one hand, thoughts were bombarding his head to make this kid suffer, and on the other was: is any of this real? What if it is all just a charade concocted by Sloane back in the cave? Robert then thought, what if he took a trip to New Mexico after the funeral to check if Sloane was there, carrying out some bizarre experiment on him, or at least he might wake up from this nightmare.

The night passed, and Robert felt numb. Numb over Jessica crying all night and numb because he was unsure what to do next. One thing was certain: Reverend Brooks was scheduled to pay the Emerson couple a visit. Considering that he had witnessed the murder of Brooks in the true reality, this was making the day more tense. As the long morning passed, he sat in his armchair staring at a picture of his family on the mantelpiece. Angelica couldn't be more than five years old at the time. He thought how meticulous Sloane was to get every fine detail so attentively in this mosaic that both perplexed and confused Robert's sense of reality and his place in the world.

The doorbell chimed at the Emerson house. Robert picked himself up from the armchair and answered it. He saw a very solemn Reverend Brooks on the other side. "Rob, what can I say?" Brooks said very compassionately.

"Please, Theodore, come inside."

Robert gestured to Brooks to take a seat near him while Jessica came into the living room carrying a tray with a pot of coffee and biscuits. The reverend gestured that he didn't want anything to eat, as his wife was recently advising him to cut down on junk food. They discussed the funeral arrangements, and Jessica was quiet. She was always a private person. She then excused herself and retreated to Angelica's room to be alone, leaving the two men in an awkward situation.

Reverend Brooks was never a man to beat around the bush and decided there and then to spit out the issue of the elephant in the room. "Rob, I know what I said to you at our last meeting. I banned you from the church. I think, under the circumstances, that I should offer you a chance to come back, considering these awful circumstances."

"Thank you, Theodore. That really says a lot to me that you are allowing me to say goodbye to my daughter."

Brooks became puzzled. He had known the micro universe's version of Robert Emerson for quite some time now, and the aberrant behaviour this man had demonstrated to him last week was very concerning. "Why did you say those nasty things to me last week and before that?"

Robert Emerson froze. He couldn't answer him because he

had no answer. Up until recently, since he arrived in this reality, that's what he was—a racist and hater. All he could think of was back in his own reality, the prime, truest of universes, that shaped him into that person. The things flowing through his mind were the day when the Exterminator murdered Brooks's counterpart and how he watched on and did nothing.

"There must be some explanation for it, dammit!"

Robert grimaced with shame. Brooks picked up on this and looked him right in the eye.

"I watched you die by my own hand."

Brooks was alarmed and becoming increasingly concerned. "Are you threatening me? Is this some kind of threat?"

"No. You're not in danger. I just want you to know how sorry I am for being such a miserable coward."

Brooks stood up and walked towards the door to let himself out. He didn't understand what Robert was saying, but put it down to his daughter's death. "I'm sorry about Angelica. See you at her funeral."

Robert couldn't sleep that night and tried to read the paper in his armchair. Jessica came down the stairs as she was unable to sleep too. He asked her to join him. They hadn't spoken to each other much since the terrible news of their daughter's death. Jessica had spent the day and evening crying and subconsciously needed a reprieve from the inner turmoil. She seated herself near her husband at the edge of the sofa. Robert became regretful and uttered something, which was indecipherable to Jessica, aloud.

"What was that?"

"She told me that she was being called names by the other kids at school."

"And you didn't think to tell me?"

"I thought nothing of it at the time. I mean, how could anyone want to hurt Angelica in any way? The mere thought of something heinous like that wouldn't enter my mind in a billion years."

"Oh, Rob. I wish you'd said something," Jessica said as she stood up and hurried up the stairs, weeping.

Robert later went into their bedroom and watched his beloved wife sleeping sadly. He began to run his fingers through her hair and also began to speak softly to her. "My sweet darling. I wasn't always the man you've come to know as me now. I was a hateful, detestable person who despised ordinary decent people, all because I felt small and shunned. When I was a boy, I thought I hadn't the right look because of my handicap, and I projected the other kids' scornful comments onto my own self-worth. My father would comment on 'perfect' people we saw on TV commercials and would mock them in derogatory ways just to make me feel better. As I grew older, I hated when people pitied me. It used to make me so angry, so I took out this anger and inflicted pain on these 'perfect' people and others weaker than me. All this, the reason as to why I was sent here, is my punishment."

Jessica fell asleep as he was telling her this. He was unsure if she'd completely heard him.

Two days later, Angelica was buried in the local cemetery. Her funeral was difficult for both her parents, especially her mother, but for her dad, Robert, it all seemed too surreal. The fact that he had only known her for over a week and the whole notion of the micro universe seemed to him now as a highfalutin construct. He wasted no more time and decided. That day, he booked a train to New Mexico. He told Jessica he was going to spend some time with distant relatives while she spent a couple of weeks with her sister.

Robert had no way of tracking down the micro universe's Sloane. He called the Grande Hotel yesterday, but they had never heard of him. This was the only course of action to make sure if he really existed here or not. As Robert was having a cup of coffee on the train, a strange-looking man in his thirties approached him and asked, "Do you mind if I take a seat?"

Robert gazed around the train and saw all the seats were occupied. What could he say or do but, "Sure. Be my guest."

This strange-looking man that Robert named the 'Weird Man' in his head offered today's newspaper to him. As Robert started reading the headlines, this man spoke. "The man you are seeking here cannot be trusted! Look at me beyond my disguise!"

This Weird Man changed into an alien being, like the one that came into his mind during the MRI scans. Robert stopped reading and looked up, but the Weird Man was nowhere to be seen. It was as if he had vanished or was never there in the first place.

A lot of time hence, however, the journey from Cleveland to New Mexico this time around seemed shorter to Robert. Perhaps because he hadn't had Sloane chattering into his ear, annoying him. He made his way to the Jornada del Muerto Desert and found the arched stone outside the cave, just like in the prime universe. Everything was the same here too, only there were no signs of campsites or anything like that. When Robert walked closer to its entrance, he noticed it hadn't made any efforts to conceal itself. He grew quite unsure whether anything or anyone was even in there. He took out his torch and switched it on. He shone it around and moved closer inside until he reached the chamber. There was similar computer equipment like in the cave in the prime universe, however, there was a strange-looking apparatus in the corner that pulsated light through the cave's ceiling. Robert looked up and immediately noticed how the ray of light seemed to penetrate the ceiling and didn't reflect off it in any way.

His concentration was soon broken when he heard particles of sediment fall, creating a dusty haze that made him cough. "Who's there?!" he asked in a low voice.

"You must be him?" a voice said.

Robert quickly turned around and saw it was indeed Sloane, or his alternate. "Sloane, I honestly didn't expect to find you here. Strange things have been happening to me ever since I got here."

"So you are really from the other side, eh?"

"Yes."

Sloane smirked and replied, "Remarkable! Tell me, is it visible in the sky at night on the other side?"

"Is what?"

"The cloud caused by the nova of the Betelgeuse star."

"Oh, the Anomaly. Yes, it is, and you can see it in the daytime too."

"Truly remarkable. What is your name?"

Robert thought that he knew his identity. "Don't you know?"

"My counterpart is only capable of communicating with me for limited periods of time. If you please?"

"Robert Emerson. And if you have already spoken to the real Sloane, then I presume you told him to bring me here? Well, I'm all ears."

Sloane moved away from Robert and didn't reply, much to the ire of Robert. He pushed Sloane up against the cave wall and pulled out his penknife. "No more games, you hear? I want to know what I'm doing here or order your counterpart to wake me up back in the real cave!"

The alternate Sloane smirked and laughed a girlish laugh. "It's quite simple, you know. I brought you here with the help of little green men, or little grey men to be precise. They helped me, and in turn, I helped the other me by fooling him. You see, it's all quite simple: we can utilize the best of both worlds and take over the prime world. I needed a sucker to be fooled so you could come here and prove to me that there is indeed another side. You're going to help me whether you like it or not."

Robert grazed Sloane's neck, and blood seeped from his skin. He was not having any of this and, after the week he had, was not going to take any more crap from the fretting idiot in front of him. "I want out of here. Instruct the other you to wake me up!"

"Not so fast. I'm not done with you yet! You see, you're just a loser, a hater. I can make your flaws become virtues for us both to prosper."

Robert had heard enough. He pushed alternate Sloane to the emitter, damaging it while it was still pulsating through the cave. Sloane yelled, "No, you idiot! You'll destroy everything! That beam is not supposed to target normal space, only the same area as where the Anomaly is in the prime universe!"

Sloane tried to pick himself up from the corner of the cave. Robert charged towards him, pointing the penknife at his chest. He stabbed him. A cry was exhorted from Sloane's lungs, followed by his dead eyes closing for the final time. Robert went over to the emitter to try to place it back in its original position; however, he noticed a strange distortion erupting out of thin air. What he saw was dark nothingness expanding and consuming the matter of the micro universe. He decided to get the hell as far away as possible from the cave and return to Cleveland. Everything here was about to die, he thought, as there was a cloud consisting of pure oblivion eating up this reality, the micro universe.

CHAPTER
NINE

Robert felt strange. He noticed how everybody else here in the micro-universe appeared oblivious to the destruction of their reality. It was as if they didn't see the distortion—more to the point, had no interaction with it at all —just being swallowed up into non-existence by it. Even his very limited knowledge of science couldn't help him even summarise a convoluted explanation for what was going on, so he decided to blend in and not do anything out of the ordinary. Here in Santa Fe, he boarded the next train to Cleveland and wanted to be with Jessica before they were all swallowed up. He stared out of the side windows and watched and waited, finally closing his eyes, trying to get some valuable sleep before he ironically woke up from whatever he was residing in.

"Excuse me, sir," a voice said.

Robert reopened his eyes and saw it was again the same Weird Man standing in front of him once again.

"Can I take a seat?" this strange man asked.

"Of course, you can, and you can also explain to me just what the hell is going on?" Robert asked, frustrated.

"It's the micro-universe; it's being consumed by oblivion. We can't stop it. You must return to Universe Prime and finish your work that you began here."

"Just what is it that you all expect me to do?"

The Weird Man sighed. "It's quite simple, really. Find the Ethereal Nebula."

Robert became almost hysterical and cried, "Just what is the 'Ethereal Nebula'?"

"It is the sole reason as to why the Anomaly was created."

Robert looked like a man who had had enough of this kind of mumbo jumbo. "No way! Find some other idiot to do your handy work! I'm out!"

The Weird Man struck Robert across the jaw, and he felt the impact with sharp, icy pain on his face. "Now you listen here!" he cried.

But the Weird Man moved in closer toward him and stared into his eyes. "Robert Emerson, it is you who must listen, and please listen carefully. The people who I protect are counting on me to protect the Ethereal Nebula. A being, like me—an alien—is intent on destroying it. We can't let that happen. You will assist us!"

Just then, the Weird Man made a very strange gesture with his hands, and electrical energy emitted from his fingers. He projected this energy toward Robert's head. Robert writhed in pain and screamed. He woke up! He was back in the actual cave in the Prime Universe.

"Robert, are you ok? I thought you were on your merry way," said Sloane.

"How long was I out?"

"Just a few seconds. I think I'm going to have to begin the transfer process again."

"No need. Because it worked. I spent weeks in the micro-universe."

Sloane was surprised to hear that but found it not inconceivable. "Really, what have you found out?"

Robert became suddenly furious and pulled the tubes from him. "You expect me to trust you? Damnit, I encountered your evil double there, and he hadn't the best intentions, I can tell you that."

Sloane knew this was a possibility. "Sorry to hear that. But I want you to know if I was in any way malevolent, I could have pulled the plug on you at any time. I'll let you get some rest, and then we'll talk."

"No way, Sloane! I'm finished with this charade. I'm going home. I've had enough!"

Later on in the cave, Sloane had checked Robert's vitals and prepared him a fresh meal. "You say this extraterrestrial told you to check for something called the 'Ethereal Nebula'?"

"Yeah, Sloane. What of it?" asked Robert, irritated.

"I wonder, could it be the Anomaly that he was talking about?"

"No, I don't think so. He told me it was the 'sole reason as to why the Anomaly was created in the first place'."

Sloane became infuriated deep within himself. He grew ever more perplexed at the meaning of all that Robert had told him earlier tonight. "We must find out more. Tomorrow we will wait here to see if this being shows up. You already said you saw him around here previously. It's logical to assume he will be back."

Robert stood up and threw the half-empty plate against the cave wall. "Don't you hear me? You're gonna have nothing to do with this no more! The evil double of you probably told you more than you're letting on. For all I know, you could be just as bad as he!"

Sloane stood up also. "Listen here, Emerson, I'm as much

in the dark as you! I honestly thought it was my AI computer program making the calculations and not my so-called *'evil double!'* I'm all you've got. It's too late now for us to split up."

With those words from Sloane's mouth no sooner said, they both heard someone entering the cave. They remained silent, and Sloane almost had a heart attack when he saw who it was. Robert knew exactly who it was – it was the Weird Man.

Sloane reluctantly approached him, much to the disconcertment of this being. Robert pulled Sloane back and moved a few inches closer to this being. "What do you want from us?" he asked him.

The Weird Man replied softly, "This man here, Edgar Sloane, is a fraud. Because he learned the truth as to how he obtained the special knowledge that brought us together, he is now being seduced by the fact that he must become like his nefarious double; otherwise, he has no purpose. You can't trust him, and therefore you must eliminate him."

"What?! *'Eliminate me'*? I'm crucial to everything going on here!" cried Sloane as he felt a cold, piercing blade impact his back. He turned around, saw Robert's unapologetic face, then fell to the stony ground.

"I'll be in touch, Mister Emerson," said the Weird Man as he vanished from sight.

Robert later buried Sloane's body and deliberately damaged all of his computer equipment. He headed back to Ohio and thought about nothing else but the next time he would encounter this Weird Man again.

After a considerable time making his way back to Cleveland, Robert was finally home, back in his real house where he was never married to Jessica, nor had they had a daughter. It was as if all those events that transpired in the now dead micro-universe were nothing but a dream. He was beginning to think everything that had happened since he witnessed Brook's murder at the hands of the Exterminator was all in his head. He believed that he was psychotic and having a nervous breakdown. His house was the same as he had left it, untidy and everything disorganized. He remembered he hadn't finished the bottle of scotch in his cupboard, so he went straight for it and, of course, imbibed. He dozed off but didn't dream of being anywhere else this time, just normal dreaming. Suddenly the doorbell chimed, and Robert awoke abruptly. He stubbornly got up and opened it to see who it was. The Exterminator greeted him with sarcastic words which he couldn't make out.

"What do you want?" asked Robert.

"Where have you been? Did you know the heat's on me? I've been calling you for weeks!"

"I was outta town, and I suggest you do the same now."

"To do that I need more money. After all, to assassinate one of the state's most prominent black leaders was all your idea."

"I don't have it!" Robert yelled as he tried to make sense of everything. Then the image of Jessica and Angelica crossed his mind, particularly Angelica. He thought of her broken, defiled body in the garage that day. He turned to the Exterminator and said, "I'll give you your money provided you do one more job for me."

"Money upfront or nothing!"

"OK, I'll give you some now and the rest on completion."

"Who this time, Emerson, the reverend's wife?"

"No, not her. I want to make some kid suffer. Put him through hell like the way he did to someone very close to me."

"If you have some of the money upfront, then yes. What's this kid's name?"

"Billy McIntyre."

"Oh, that's his name?" the Exterminator asked as he reached for a small gun in his right pocket.

"Make him regret the day he was born," said Robert unsuspectingly.

"Billy's my nephew!" the Exterminator yelled as he tried to push Robert inside the house. Robert managed to push him and kicked the gun from his hand. Then he kicked him in the stomach, but the Exterminator was much younger than he, and got up quickly and punched Robert in the face. He was bruised on the left of his face. The Exterminator picked up the gun and pointed it at Robert. "Any final words, Emerson?"

Robert managed to knee the Exterminator in the groin with a show of final strength. He fell to the ground, winded. Robert snatched the gun and blew the Exterminator's head off – almost. Another one dead and another reason for hopelessness, and something else to eat at Robert Emerson's soul.

As Robert tied up everything, he knew both the Exterminator's people and his own would be coming for him. He had to leave this time for good. He disposed of the body and packed his things. As he was about to open the front door and exit his home for the last time, he was confronted with the sudden appearance of the Weird Man.

"Not now! I've to get outta here!"

"There is only one place you can safely go to, and that's with me," replied the Weird Man.

Robert grew more panicky, "Look! They're looking for me. All of my past sins have caught up with me."

"And in the future, you will find redemption. Acquiesce to me."

Robert thought for a moment, and more moments passed. He looked up at the Weird Man, who was strangely staring down at him, and nodded his head. The Weird Man formed a sphere of light when he put the palms of his hands together, and this sphere transformed into an orb. He handed the orb to Robert, and it began to glow and then pulsate until he was completely shrouded in light. Robert then vanished.

To be concluded...

ABOUT THE AUTHOR

John Paul Warren was born on June 12, 1975 in Ireland. He writes passionately in his free time about characters who are pulled into ethical dilemmas and use personal introspection to solve their problems and usually references on our ever so strange human condition.

———

To learn more about John P. Warren and discover more Next Chapter authors, visit our website at www.nextchapter.pub.

Underneath the Surreal Starshine
ISBN: 978-4-82419-822-8

Published by
Next Chapter
2-5-6 SANNO
SANNO BRIDGE
143-0023 Ota-Ku, Tokyo
+818035793528

24th September 2024

www.ingramcontent.com/pod-product-compliance
Lightning Source LLC
LaVergne TN
LVHW090039080526
838202LV00046B/3875